MW01593933

No Body,
No Crime

— just can't prove it

BY ELIŠKA BELEJOVÁ

"*I think he did it but I just can't prove it*
No, no body, no crime
But I ain't letting up until the day I die
No, no
I think he did it
No, no
He did it."

INDEX

Authors Note

I'm a firm believer that music holds the biggest power to inspire, and that it tells a story. No matter what the song may be about, if you listen to the lyrics you can see the tape playing out in your mind, a story that the song is talking about.

Of course from those few opening lines, you probably think this will be a beautiful story with a happy ending. I hate to crush your dreams but no. From the title you can probably guess; yes, it's a crime short.

Speaking of the title, it might sound familiar. This story is not only inspired by a song but is completely based on it's lyrics.

This detective, crime short story follows the twisted mind of Este's sister Danielle - or Taylor? And the twisted secrets that erupt into chaos in

the secure, modest town that was Kohler,
Wisconsin.

Preface

November had laid a cozy blanket of snow over the small town of Kohler where nothing ever happened. The police station was more like the reception desk in an old hotel on route 66 that no one ever visits anymore, than a group of officers that are meant to fight crime. But no one ever complained. After all, why would they? Having no crime in your town is only good for you as a sheriff and a precinct.

Like they had in routine, Danielle and Este always met at Tim's diner precisely at ten fifteen every Tuesday morning for breakfast and catch up on their week past. On Tuesdays both girls started work late and used their free mornings to voice their recent agenda as well as the town's recent happenings. Gossip was a regular theme in their conversations. Kohler was a small town of only two thousand people but to those who lived there it felt like just one long windy street where everyone knew everyone and their business. Keeping secrets in such a town was hard. But neither the Sheriff, nor Danielle ever thought they would have secrets. And they never expected one of the most innocent people to be involved in such a dirty business as the one that infected the community in November of 2020.

The Sheriff's onto Danielle. Who is Taylor? Danielle knows what Dan has done. Este is dead.

He did it.

Part 1

Smells Like Infidelity

Este was still brushing her hair with her fingers when she walked across the street to Tim's Diner. Her dirty blond hair blew in the wind, making it impossible to get that ponytail to work. She pushed the door of the restaurant open with her right foot and walked over to Taylor who was already sipping on her coffee.

"You look like you haven't slept in 10 years."

"Why, good morning to you too." Este said sarcastically. She bit down on her hair tie brushing her hair into a ponytail once again. As she was about to loop her hair through the tie one more time, it snapped where it was connected. Finally Este gave up and let her hair down naturally before letting out a growl of frustration.

"Not your day?" Este shook her head no and Taylor rubbed her shoulder over the table. "Hey Tim, one black coffee over here! Oh and a refill!" Taylor shouted to the bartender.

"I haven't slept all night." Este finally sighed. "I think Dan's cheating on me..."

"How so?"

"I found lipstick in his car... It was nude as well." Taylor's eyes went wide. Este never wore nude lipstick. Never. Her colour was red. Only red.

The bell above the restaurant door went ding dong again just as they'd finished speaking. Danielle, Este's sister came and joined the door at the booth by the window. The snow outside was getting heavier by the looks of it; Danielle had a trail of melting snow behind her, and the water was still dripping down her black leather jacket.

"Dan's cheating on Este." Taylor said abruptly, greeting Danielle.

"What do you mean?" Danielle put down all her things, getting cozy in her seat.

"She means there was nude lipstick in Dan's car and money keeps "mysteriously" disappearing from our bank account. He says it's all the jewelry he's bought me. Which is another thing, he keeps buying me all these prissy jewels for no reason. I took some of the stuff to the pawnbrokers the other day and Sally said none of those things are worth more than $20."

Taylor and Este looked at eachother, both of their stares worrying Este just a little.

"You have a raving look in your eyes. Both of you." She laughed.

"I think I'm gonna call him out." Taylor finally said. The entire situation smelled of infidelity and Taylor was determined to do something about it. Este wasn't very fond of that. Dan was already suspecting that Este was onto him and he wasn't one you'd want to cross ways with when he's mad. Este would be lying if she said he hadn't hit her in the past or got violent when he got angry, or even that he threatened her with death. The last thing she'd want is for her friends to get in the way. Who knows what he'd do; who knows who he'd hit this time. But Taylor was resilient and Danielle had her back. The three were lost in thought for a moment only to be taken back to reality by Stella bringing their food and a bottle of wine.

"I always knew having a joint account wouldn't be a good idea. It never is a good idea." Danielle spoke up, thinking about personal experiences. "You should learn from my mistakes lil' sis'."

"Yeah I know… I'd still rather you didn't do anything though. You know what he's like…" Este replied, growing quieter with every word.

In the small town in Illinois that was Kohler, everyone knew everyone and their business - well more or less. Stella, Tim and Sally all went to school with Danielle, Este and Taylor. Dan moved to Kohler in 2011 when he and Este got married after meeting each other in Chicago over the summer. The whole thing was very sudden but that was Este's nature and her intuition had never failed her before so no one really questioned it. Apparently, Dan moved to Kohler because he was sick of the city. Well that's what he said anyway. He's always been the odd sheep in the community. Sally once swore she saw him walking around town with an axe at night; She was closing up the shop one night in late August so the days were getting shorter by the day. It was already dark when she saw him and according to her tall-tale-mouth of gossip he was lurking around the streets looking angrier than anyone had ever seen him. The following day, they found out there was some truth to it after the sheriff got a call from Mr Gibson that one of his dear cows was slaughtered in the night. (The trail of blood leading from the farm to halfway through the town centre where Sally saw him didn't do good to his name either). Sally and the others thought he did it but she just couldn't prove it. It became even more suspicious when Este said that he came home late that night saying he went out to rid himself of his anger which he was suppressing for months - Este's arm bruise from three days before didn't agree with his alibi. Este thought he did it too, but she also couldn't prove it. There were other strange things that had happened over the nine years Dan lived in Kohler that all pointed to him, but Dan was not one to be messed with and the sheriff couldn't exactly do anything about him either - mainly because he was already 76 and walking with a cane, but also because there wasn't enough evidence for anything. They just couldn't prove that it was him.

-Part 2-

Goodbye Este

That night when Este got home after having dinner with her sister and Taylor at the diner, Dan was acting more suspicious than ever before. His breath stunk of alcohol and the almost empty, open bottle of Merlot in the kitchen just proved Este's theory that he was drinking to be true. Este asked him why he was drinking alone, and hinted at whether he really was alone before she got home. He ignored her completely, turning the situation around and finding some petty thing to argue about that could be blamed on her instead. The lipstick on his neck spoke for everything. His tactic of arguing worked, setting Este up for yet another sleepless night of tears and the rest of the Merlot to herself. At one point she got up to pack her things and leave for good, but the thought of what Dan could do when he figured it out in the morning frightened her. When she finished the bottle of Merlot she felt sick to her stomach- and not from the alcohol.

The lip mark on his neck, the open bottle, it all led to the one obvious thing. She wondered who his mistress was, and then she realized she drank from the same bottle another woman had drank from with her husband before. A memory from their wedding played on loop in Este's head. She remembered how they vowed to never leave each other standing alone, how they would love each other unconditionally. Now he's ripped her heart out of her chest and dropped it; let it smash like glass. Este's cheeks were soon drenched in her own salty tears that she couldn't hold back anymore. The agony had overpowered her and she threw the now-empty bottle of wine to the floor. The glass shattered on the floor, and her tears just got more intense by the moment. Este started picking up the shards of glass and throwing them in the bin. One piece was particularly sharp, cutting the palm of her hand - blood was dripping all over the floor. She clutched her hand in a fist to stop it but the blood leaked through her fingers. Light came from the hallways and she soon realized she had woken up Dan. The emotional state she was in wasn't anything Dan's seen before and he wasn't having it. Anger bought out a side of her no one's ever experienced before and she decided to embrace it. There was no doubt Dan would get more angry than ever, but Este was determined to let him know exactly how she feels.

"What the hell are you doing?" Dan rubbed his eyes, already burning up that he had to wake up at one in the morning.

"How could you? After everything I've put up with for the past nine years, all the threats and bruises and you cheat on me like I'm nothing?" Este screamed, ignoring whatever he said. "Haven't you got *any* decency at all? All the shit you put me through…" She stopped at the kitchen counter to bandage her hand. "Everything you've ever done to me, I forgave you for. *Everything*. This is your thank you?" She stormed over to him beating at his chest. "How could you - how could you- *how could you*?" Tears flowed right out of her eyes, her drunken state draining her energy faster than normal as she tucked hard at the collar of his shirt. "You know, deep down I still hoped... I still had a glimmer of belief in my heart that you could change; that it would all turn out fine in the end. Any other woman would have left you despite your threats, but you brainwashed me. You manipulated me into thinking you were the good guy even though it was out in plain sight that you're the villain. You made me believe everything was okay. You made me your slave and I thanked you! I did anything you asked of me and this is how you repay me?" Her screams were half-muffled by the tears she choked on as she beat at his chest and he tried to stop her.

Dan grabbed hold of Este's arms, trying to stop her. His actions were (not surprising and) way more aggressive than they should be such a situation. Este kept trying to wiggle out of his grip but she couldn't, despite all her attempts his hold on her was much too tight.

What followed in Este's fate was nothing she would have imagined nor wanted. Threats are one thing, they're plain words that are easy to speak. The actions that correspond to those words are much harder, yet not even Este thought Dan would do anything of the sort.

It was one in the morning, in late October. The moon was high up in the sky and there was nothing to be seen unless you stood under the streetlights. Dan had had enough. After all he had a new target now. Natalie didn't know anything about him. The fake innocency he threw on around her had his mistress fooled. She was clueless.

He was done with Este, he had drained her all he could. So what now?

He slapped Este across the face, throwing her to the floor where she cut herself on the broken glass even more. She looked at him through angry tears, careless, and punched him in the face. Dan fell back, and Este stayed sitting amongst the broken bottle pieces, lacking energy to even move.

"You shouldn't have done that."

Este looked at him, giving him the side eye while she tried to catch her breath. He caught it sooner. Dan picked her up and dragged her out of the kitchen. One of the last things she saw was the inside of the car trunk with her hands and legs tied behind her and a rag in her mouth. He drove her to the outskirts of the town, and stopped at a small cliff side by the lake. Este shouted and cried, but the fabric in her mouth muffled her screams for help before anyone could hear her. Dan threw her onto the ground, untying her, giving her the false hope of getting away. Este tried to run, but her legs failed her, numb from the long car ride.

"This isn't how you were supposed to go, but you gave me no choice." The axe in his hand left a trail in the dirt as he dragged it behind him. The last thing Este saw was the blade of an exe glinting in the moonlight before her eyes became clouded by the dark, cold water of the lake.

-Part 3-

Intuition

Taylor and Danielle sat at their usual booth at Tim's but both of them were on the edge of their seat. Neither of the two have heard from Este since last Tuesday and they felt uneasy. The two clutched their mugs of coffee in their hands to warm up from the biting cold outside. Danielle was staring out into the abyss, the people outside the window thinking she was staring at them. She was thinking about all the possible scenarios of why Este hasn't called, why she wasn't at work, just why? Why wasn't Este there? Taylor had her suspicions too; both of them did. Everyone else that knew Este was thinking the same thing.

"Refill?" Stella came by their table. The two nodded. "Where's Este?" They shrugged.

"We don't know." Danielle said.

"We've got our suspicions… And they all lead to Dan." Taylor added.

Stella didn't question any of it and went on to serve the other customers. Taylor had a hunch. She thought it was far fetched at first but she decided that it was a likely possibility rather than an impossible occurrence.

"Dan did it. I'm certain of it." Taylor suddenly blurted out, snapping Danielle out of her daze.

"What?"

"I said Dan did it. There's no other explanation." You could say Taylor was jumping to conclusions, after all that's what Danielle was thinking too. Not that it was too hard to believe that Dan's last screw finally went loose, she just couldn't bring herself to actually think that her sister was in another life - or rather without one, and that it all happened at the hands of her own husband. Danielle remained sitting, staring into space with tears prying themselves out of her eyes but Taylor was already gathering her stuff and putting her coat on. Eventually Danielle snapped out of her trance and followed Taylor out into the chilly October streets of Kohler. She was about to question where they were going until Taylor turned to cross the street and walked straight towards the pawnbrokers.

Sally was the keeper of all gossip about town. She knew *everything* about *everyone*, which is why it was also no surprise to the girls when she skipped the formalities upon their arrival and went straight to the topic of where Este has gone to. Every afternoon, on her way to the Diner, Este would drop off a piece of pie, or cookies or whatever it is that she baked on Monday morning.

"Is Este alright? No ones seen her all week - since last Tuesday it's like she's just disappeared."
And Sally was right, it seemed like she had gone off the grid completely. Sally got no cake, Tim didn't serve her morning coffee at all for the past seven days, Mrs Crowley had to open the library herself... Everyone was asking the same thing. Where was Este?

Taylor also went straight to the point.

"No, she's not alright at all. In fact I don't think she *is* at all." To this comment even Shane, Sally's husband reacted, turning away from rearranging the display behind the counter. Sally and Shane looked at each other worriedly. Danielle shared the same look. Then her gaze suddenly fell on something glinting behind Sally in a box that was labeled "to price and display."

"That axe…"

Sally turned around, looking in the direction Danielle was looking.

"Oh yes. Dan bought this here this morning. Said he doesn't want it anymore - apparently "his days with an axe are over." You can interpret that however you want but I decided to not interpret it at all." Sally explained picking it up and putting it on the counter. Danielle just nodded. No emotion on her face or in her heart, she suddenly grew cold and revengeful

"He did it. And I ain't letting up until the day he dies." Taylor put a hand on her shoulder.

"Neither am I. And we'll get to the bottom of this. I promise you that. He'll get what he deserves. But…" Taylor stopped in her tracks as to not seem so abrupt. "We might need some help." She looked at Sally and Shane. The married couple shared a look once again and asked the girls to join them for dinner with a *count-us-in* smile when another customer walked into the shop.

Taylor and Danielle took their goodbyes and walked out of the shop, towards the library. Danielle was growing redder by the minute and had an incredible urge to stop Dan's existence right then. Taylor of course stopped her and told her to be her good old, rational self;

that they'll need her intelligent brain and good memory. Once they reached the library they went straight to the main desk. Mrs Crowley was sorting through some books on a nearby book stack.

"Oh hello girls, how nice to see you here." She exclaimed happily, peeking through a gap in the shelf. Mrs Crowley climbed down the ladder and went over to the girls. She was an elderly lady, but energetic and active nonetheless. She was more like a grandma to everyone in the town than just the local librarian. "How can I help you?"

"Good afternoon Mrs Crowley. We were just wondering, when was the last time you saw Este?"
The librarian thought for a moment to make sure she had gotten the date right.

"Oh yes that must have been last Tuesday dear. I haven't seen her since. She looked very upset that day too. After she went to have dinner with you both she came back here, saying she couldn't bear to see her husband just yet. She went home very late - well it's late on my watch but I suppose ten in the evening isn't so late for your generation." She laughed. Danielle thanked her and they walked out again.

"Do you think he really sold the axe because-" Danielle cut her off.

"I don't know but I don't really want to think about that. I also don't know where you're going now because I'm going to go talk to the sheriff. Dan most definitely didn't do it so I will." Taylor wanted to protest, knowing that Este wouldn't have gone off the grid on purpose. It was the sad truth that Este was dead and Taylor was slowly beginning to accept she would never see her again, but her sister still hoped and she couldn't take that away from Danielle.

Part 4

The Plan

After the pair reported Este as missing and asked some more around town, they headed back towards the diner to Taylors car. On their way to Sally and Shane's house, Danielle had the idea to drive past Este and Dan's house to see if there was anything suspicious that could help them.

"So what do you propose we do?" Shane sat down in the arm chair with a bottle of beer.

"Let's put it this way; rich parents sometimes are a win after all; my dad made me get a boating license when I was fifteen. It's also a good thing that you two took shifts next Saturday and Shane went home early because you were feeling sick - which is why the shop was closed early. Also Tim served you some chicken soup to go - We'll have to talk to him about that later. Of course Este's sister's gonna swear she was with me - because I'm not letting anyone apart from myself get into the list of suspects. Also, it's a good thing Dan's mistress took out a big life insurance policy."

"How do you know that?" Sally questioned.

"I got my ways."

But the truth was that Taylor saw a list of life insurance withdrawals from the past week at the council office when she went to work the previous day. As a lawyer she dealt with tonnes of different things around the town.

And it was when she was thinking about exactly this when it hit her.

"Oh my God." She half shouted. "This is perfect." Everyone sort of just started at her blankly not knowing what she was talking about.

"I'm a lawyer. No one would ever suspect the lawyer."

Taylor got a few awkward glances from the others in response to her statement but somehow they all came to an agreement in the end. Shane was still slightly skeptical though.

"Okay so back to my original question. What do you propose we do?" Shane killed the silence. Taylor actually hadn't thought that far ahead, all she knew that he deserved what he had done to her beloved sister.

"We're going to give him a taste of his own medicine. There's no doubt he used that axe he took to your shop, and we all know that his mistress has already moved in and Este's barely bean de- she's hardly been gone for a week. Either he did it all for her so he could use her, or she made him do it - but that in my opinion is a very long stretch. I've met a few psychopaths in my life and deal with killers on the daily. She doesn't strike me as that type from the little I've seen of her around the town."

"So we use an axe?" Shane questioned further.

"No. We use *his* axe." Sally corrected him.

"I like your thinking Sal. We'll leave it for a few more days, say until Friday, to observe them and when we're certain of our theory, we'll give him a sweet weekend he'll never forget." Taylor grinned like none of them had ever seen before.

"Now that's a maniacal grin." Sally laughed to lighten the mood.

"Sure is." Shane joined in, getting up to grab a glass of whisky.

For the next few hours the four of them didn't pick up their phones, ignored any outside interactions and focused on noting down and making sense of everything they knew of what happened after Este's death. They went over everything from the most obvious to anything that possibly be even remotely related to the murder.

Taylor was living out her detective dream, but she never let it show. Obviously that would have been more than beyond inappropriate. She was a lawyer yes, so technically she was still in that type of field (sort of) but her true calling has always been the criminal investigation service. Ever since she was a little girl she's wanted to be a CIA agent, a detective or even a sheriff at the worst. But the real worst thing that happened was that even though she got accepted to the police academy her parents were set on her going off to study law and she has always regretted not standing up for herself more when they sent her away to law school.

"Wait, I saw him drive up to the lake last week. I'm actually pretty sure it was on Tuesday night." Shane stopped the girls in their tracks.

"What were you doing by the lake last Tuesday?" Sally asked him, now annoyed and clueless as to why he was out late at night by the lake. "Were you *with* someone?" Danielle and Taylor didn't feel this awkward in a long time.

"No." He rolled his eyes, equally annoyed at her reaction. "You sent me there to get our ladder back from Michael because you wanted something from the attic and he borrowed it the week before. Remember?"

"Oh…"

"Sheriff's calling." Danielle suddenly stood up. Taylor held her hand, looking at her sympathetically.

Danielle picked up the call with shaky hands. It took her four tries to slide her finger across the screen and actually answer the Sheriff. She answered with a simple hello when she felt tears hold back her words. She put the phone on speaker.

"Danielle, I'm so sorry… We've just found a body in the lake. We think it's Este… But we need you to identify her… I'm so sorry."

Danielle threw the phone across the room, falling into Taylors hug. Sally picked up her phone and answered the Sheriff telling him they would be there in a few minutes."

-Part 5-

The Funeral

When the group arrived at the scene they were met by more police officers than anyone of them - potentially except Taylor - had ever seen and an oh-so-pretty "CRIME SCENE DO NOT CROSS" tape. Danielle couldn't ever bring herself to step out of the car. She would soon drown in her own tears if the other three didn't offer her hands to hold and shoulders to lean on.

Her sister, well her body was thankfully easily identifiable, but that's needless to say that they all still wished they didn't see their sweet librarian with blood stained clothes, lungs full of water and an open skull - or that's what the initial first look autopsy said at least. Danielle kneeled down next to the body of her sister in the dirt by the lake. She looked at her lovingly and said under her breath:

"We will give him what he deserves, Este. He'll pay for this."

"Damn right we will." The Sheriff put his hand on Danielle's shoulder. "He'll get locked up for what he's ever done. We'll take care of him, don't you worry about that." He looked at the group of four, unaware they were already planning their own revenge for Dan.

When Danielle went home that night she asked the others to join her, including Tim and Stella from the diner to help her plan the one thing she never thought she'd have to do; the thing she was scared of from the start; planning Este's funeral. And sure enough, a week later on a Tuesday afternoon Este's funeral took place at Saint John's. The amount of black Danielle saw that day made her cry even more than she wanted because it all reminded her of her Danielle & Este's parents' funeral from seven years ago.

Everyone came. Whether it was the girls' distant family, close friends, acquaintance, co-workers... Danielle could have sworn she had never seen their cousins cry so much. Even Mrs Crowley was sobbing in her son's arms and he too was crying. Taylor and their closest friends gave the most beautiful speeches. Danielle couldn't find the strength to speak so their cousin James gave his and hers too. Though one thing that angered yet not even slightly surprised the melancholy crowd was Dan. The husband and supposed murderer stood far away, merely watching the show from afar. There was no black on his clothes except the big *Nike* tick on his shirt. When Danielle and a couple of others noticed him he gave a cold stare and walked away. It was clear to everyone that he didn't care nor at least felt it appropriate to act like he shared their sorrow and grief.

Obviously due to the circumstances they decided to postpone any vengeful plans and give everyone time to absorb the cruel reality. This was unfortunately something which the four had failed to realize or note down when they planned their revenge. It was more than understandable that they all needed time and space. Even Taylor, who wasn't very emotional most of the time when it came to sadness, found herself being quite weak in the days that followed. They all shared the same red puffiness around their eyes; a shortage of tissues; no motivation; gazing into oblivion and zoning out at work. The reality had hit. It was no longer a cat and mouse chase where they were the cat sure to catch the mouse soon. The mouse was on the loose, enjoying his life with his new mouse friend. He was perfectly content with what he had done and it was more than clear to everyone that he had no regrets.

Unfortunately life had to go on in the small town of Kohler. Tim opened and ran the diner every day, even every Tuesday, as usual with Stella and the other staff. But they all looked at that one booth where Este always sat with Danielle and Taylor every Tuesday afternoon. Shane and Sally still ran their pawnbrokers, but glared with envy at the axe that sat in the corner in a box untouched since Danielle asked about it a couple weeks ago. Danielle too still went to work and had to go about her life as normal. Mrs Crawley felt lonely in the library though. There was no one quietly humming in a random book isle and there were no cookies waiting for her every morning. Danielle got fed up with her days at the office and decided to fill the space that Este so unfortunately left behind. She applied for the place that Este had at the library and Mrs Crawley gladly took her in. After all there were only subtle differences between Danielle and her sister. It almost felt like Este was there still, for both of them. Taylor wasn't sick of her job, but she wanted justice. Sadly, most of her current cases reminded her of Este, and that she most definitely didn't enjoy.

Dan was unbothered. Dan was with his new girlfriend. Poor girl didn't know what she had gotten herself into when she started dating him and a lot of people were starting to feel sorry for her. She turned out to be very sweet and oblivious to what Dan had done. One day, Dan and Mary were arguing in the street between Tim's diner and the pawnbrokers.

"She was your wife?" Mary started.

"Yeah so? She was. Stop making a scene."

"So? Oh I'll give you a scene if you want one, mister. That means you were cheating on me. You arrogant piece of shit. And you didn't even go to her funeral? Do you have any decency?"

The argument carried on until Mary got back out of the car right after getting in and walking away. Dan was left in the street for everyone to laugh at because someone finally had the nerve to stand up to him.

-Part 6-

Going Solo

Taylor took matters into her own hands. She swore that she wasn't letting up until the day he died and she would keep her word. Dan was done for. So, one night about a month after Este's funeral, instead of going home after work, Taylor stopped by the pawnbrokers and asked Sally for the axe. She had obviously forgotten that the police had the axe now due to investigation on Dan and Este's murder. But Taylor couldn't take much more and was prepared to use any means to get her way. She stormed into the police station and asked permission to see the evidence room with the excuse that she was there on work conditions and needed to look into some of the evidence against the criminal. Somehow the receptionist ate the bait and let Taylor in.

Taylor slipped into the evidence storage and didn't take half as long as she anticipated she would. With more than just a little bit of struggle she stuffed the axe into her bag and made her way out of the police station as fast as she could while trying to look the least suspicious she possibly could after stealing criminal evidence from the evidence locker. She had long made up her mind that these were the last moments of her innocence. With this in mind she abruptly took her actions to a halt and drove to Tim's. She sat at the usual booth and ordered Este's usual for herself. She only thought it appropriate to see Danielle one more time before she was running from the cops. However, she had promised herself that she wouldn't tell a word of her sudden plan to anyone, not even Danielle. When Danielle got there, emotionless and numb, they had dinner like they used to and remembered all the fun times they had had together with Este. Tears were most definitely shed throughout the evening, even more so when Danielle also ordered Este's favorite meal.

In the meantime the sheriff had entered the evidence locker only to find the axe from Este's case missing. Truthful was what the receptionist said: that only two people had gone into the room that day. Those two people were Danielle and Mr Stanford, a criminal defence lawyer. The sheriff immediately called it a night done at the office for a few of the staff and they were sent out into the tiny town of two thousand people to investigate immediately.

Taylor had eventually forgotten about her initial plan and the two stayed at the diner until closing hour. Tim and Stella were the only people there at the end. They decided to sit down with Dani & Tay for a little bit and reminisce with them instead of throwing them out so they can close up the place. They even found a mark on the wall from years ago when Tim had just opened up the place again after his dad closed it up for good. Tim revived the place and gave it a fresh vibe that people loved so Este, Taylor and Danielle, being the stupid trio they always were when they were together decided they should leave their mark on the place too since they spent so much time there anyway.

Down under the windowsill was a part of the wall that was covered with the table so it wasn't very visible. Right in the middle of that wall the initials "E", "T" and "D" were etched into the paint and top layer of plaster, underlined with three lines that were each of a different length and all in a heart with an arrow through, piercing it. This condemned even more tears, not only from Tay and Dani but also from Stella and Tim.

The four high school friends proceeded to close up the diner and all go to Taylor's place. Before this however, they picked up everyone else that was in their old high school crew and ordered some food. They spent the night watching old videos and looking through photo albums, remembering Este how she would have wanted them to. She wouldn't want them to cry for hours, days on end. She always said it anyway, that she wanted them to have fun after she was gone and remember her through things she would have loved. Her lifestyle with Dan made her more comfortable with dark humour; she used it as a coping mechanism.

Taylor was reminded of her previous action plan to what happened after she went to the diner when she pulled Dan's axe out of her bag. She looked at it and hesitated. With the excuse that she was going to get wine so they can toast to Este's well deserved rest now that she doesn't have to be with a maniac like Dan. Truth was however, that Taylor was sneaking into the police station to replace the stolen evidence and she pulled it off rather well - although she did almost trigger the alarm three times in a row. She didn't however leave the station empty handed. She took the scarf Este was found wearing. It still had a little blood on it, but she took it anyway. She thought to herself, if she was going to do all of this, she would do it her way. She would get him ten times worse than he got Este.

Taylor ended up returning home with a bottle of wine from the petrol station and a clear mind, ready to reevaluate her plan of attack. For the rest of the night the group did the same things in a loop; eat, drink, videos, photos, until the last of them finally fell asleep at two in the morning.

Sheriff Steward and his team had been searching all night and everything led to only one person in the end: Taylor. It was all more than proven when two policemen saw her sneak back into the police station to return the stolen evidence.

-Part 7-

Cat and Mouse Chase

"Miss Newland..." A knock came from the door. "Miss Newland, open up." Knock number two pounded at the door.

Finally Sally woke up to the noise. Blinking the bright light away she opened the door for the policeman.

"Good Morning, is Miss Newland here?"

"Sheriff you're talking like you've never met either of us."

"Miss." The Sheriff pressed, losing his patience.

"Oh this is a serious matter. One second." Sally closed the door and went back in.

"Sheriff's here, wants to talk to Taylor..?"

The remainder of the party exchanged confused glances telling Sally that Taylor wasn't there. Although she told the Sheriff this, he wasn't satisfied with that answer and so she invited him in to see for himself, but he declined. He was on his way soon enough and the others talked about how strange that was.

"It was probably about work." Shane assured them.

And in the end it was true. Taylor wasn't there because she left early that morning to get a headstart on her plan. A note was waiting on the others on the kitchen table telling them that she was called into work early that morning, that they could help themselves to food and kindly asking them to lock the door behind them and leave the key in the tulip pot by the door.

The cat was loose, and the mouse was unsuspecting. It was a perfect opportunity to strike if only the Sheriff didn't interrupt. The most confident person in town was suddenly showered in cold sweat and she made accidental eye contact with the (probably suspecting) policeman. He questioned her for a solid half hour but she had already rehearsed her alibi and any detail she might be asked for. The sheriff eventually left empty handed. He was no less suspicious of her than before however.

Unfortunately by the time the coast was clear and no cops were in sight it was too late. Dan had seen her and was aware she was onto him. He was already sitting in his car starting the engine when she looked over at his house. Taylor walked away and waited for him to drive away. Once his truck was out of sight she crept inside the house through the back door.

First, her instinct told her to set a trap but she was a loose cannon and when the idea sparked in the fireplace that he forgot to switch off she was certain this was the way to go. Although the thought of the sheriff worried her she shook it off. He was already suspicious so be it. Whatever fate decided will be. There's no going around what destiny has planned for you so Taylor thought along the same lines. Taylor started searching the house for any type of alcohol; wine, beer (although she needed something stronger than that). Lucky her, she then discovered a bottle of whisky in the cabinet.

A thought of sudden regret hit her just before she threw the bottle in the fire. This was Este's home. She felt like a tragic character in a movie for a second while she remembered all the times the three girls spent there even before Dan joined the picture. However, revenge was revenge, and her decision was set in stone. Or, set in fire rather. She looked around one more time wondering whether there was anything she should save from the fire but upon deeper thought she'd decided that saving nothing would be better because she knew that saving one thing would make her want to take the rest.

From that moment on Taylor kept inside the shadows and didn't talk to anyone. No one had seen her at all and she wanted it exactly that way. She didn't want anyone to be seen with her and blame to be put on them when the police found her. And it was right of her to do so because the dogs weren't far behind the cat. Not to even mention the mouse was getting away.

The house was discovered burning by Dan's neighbours and he was called home immediately by his girlfriend who got called by the police when Dan wasn't picking up. Mary was panicking, wondering what had happened but the firefighters told her they couldn't tell her until the homeowner was there. It was another half hour before Dan arrived at the scene only to discover almost everything apart from the foundations of the house burned to the ground. The fire brigade was quick to find the cause of the fire and told the pair that a bottle was found in the fireplace. Mary immediately blamed Dan, knowing how much he liked to drink. Of course he denied it and was for once not lying, but Mary didn't believe him and she had a right to, knowing all the rumours that were going around town.

Dan knew well that it was Taylor that caused this, and in his dictionary this meant war. But the mouse wouldn't get very far before the cat was creeping up just round the corner again. Almost at once Dan started thinking of a plan to get rid of Taylor but knew that it would be hard. Two murders in such a small amount of time would definitely get him arrested. He had contemplated many things, thinking of a plan to get out of this mess but most of them required a confession to Mary which he couldn't do. Although at this point he was debating in his mind, whether Mary was an important part of the picture. Eventually he had made up his mind, if it had to be; Mary had to go. But his priority was Taylor, not Mary and the part she played in this.

Dan knew Taylor was onto him. Taylor knew that Dan was onto her. But neither would stand down. It was a question of life and death. It was a cat and mouse chase.

-Part 8-

Suspicions

At the police station the Sheriff was trying to set things into order and was even making the worst links imaginable - some which were the very opposite of true. He even came up with a theory that Taylor was the one to kill Este and added her to the list of suspects. Of course his speculations were very wrong but he continued to get lost in his thoughts and overlooked the possibility that was true; the possibility of revenge.

It was anything but a good wake up call but Danielle got one from the police instead of hearing her alarm an hour later. The sheriff decided to pull at all strings to see who murdered Este and was clearly very dedicated to his theory of Taylor killing her best friend because of jealousy. Danielle had no choice but to get up and be ready in twenty minutes or less before the police car showed up at her door. All she knew at that moment was that the sheriff wanted to ask a few questions about Taylor and it rather frightened her and when he arrived she found herself struggling to maintain a straight face and lashing out at the policeman after he suggested that a certain someone may have killed her sister.

"I've known Taylor my whole life. She would never lay hands on anyone."

"People change Miss Henderson."

"Well I know that Taylor hasn't. She would never hurt Este. She was her best friend. they got on even better than Taylor and myself."

"Do you think that could have been a motif?" He whipped out a notebook and pen.

"What? How could that be a motif? Sheriff, I've known you since I was a baby. My parents knew you and so did Taylors. Let's face it you know everyone in this godforsaken town and you're really suspecting Taylor of Este's murder? Are you mad? Everything leads to Dan. The clues are so obvious yet you're still somehow sitting in my living room at half past eight in the morning trying to tell me that Este's best friend killed her because they got on better than Taylor and me? Do you realize how ridiculous that sounds?"

The sheriff was practically speechless and sat in silence for a short moment.

"I have to weigh all the options, Miss-"

"Well news flash sheriff, I already have. And so has Taylor. Dan got new tyres on his truck the day after Este was supposedly murdered according to your forensics. He fucked her up emotionally, she could never sleep and he abused her but she was the strongest person I ever knew and I know she didn't throw herself into that river voluntarily and without help. Her head was almost cut in two with what was proven to be an axe; the axe that is sitting somewhere at the station probably in a plastic bag and no one has probably even looked at it since you've gotten your hands on it. That axe is Dan's. It literally has his initials engraven in the handle. That is the axe he took to the pawnbrokers also a day after Este's estimated death. Sally had it sitting in a crate at the store for a day. It was shiny like a gemstone - like it was new. Clearly he got rid of all the DNA and probably her blood that was on the steel."

"Miss Henderson-"

"No. Don't "Miss Henderson" me. You have just proven to me that an art graduate can solve the case better than a trained policeman. You can call me when you've got Dan locked up in a cell, otherwise I don't want to hear from you. Goodbye, I trust you can find the door yourself."

Danielle turned around walking to the kitchen to get a glass of water. She chugged it down in one and took a few deep breaths. Still she hadn't heard the door open or close.

"Danielle... we caught Taylor on the security tape from the evidence locker taking the axe and returning it the night you and the rest of Este's friends had a get-together." The sheriff appeared in the kitchen doorway. Danielle almost choked on her water and found herself in a coughing fit. Naturally, the sheriff helped her and she soon regained her balance and stature.

"She took the axe?" The sheriff nodded. "Have you seen Dan since then?"

"Yes." The Sheriff answered at once, sensing more suspicion. "Do you know something about this?"

"What - no! No, I had no idea she was there... I think it might be better if you go, sheriff. I need some time to think about all of this."

Finally the sheriff left, and surprisingly without any further question. However he did seem to piece together the tape and Danielle's reaction. Finally he realized that Taylor was innocent in the case of Este's murder but noted down to keep a close watch on Este's widower. He wasn't all surprised when he started noticing sceptical behaviour in Dan. He kept an eye on him and questioned everyone he could.

"Turns out this case is more complicated than anyone had anticipated."

Of course Danielle couldn't let go of what was fresh in her brain. Given the consequences, and the fact that the sheriff now *knows* she retraced all her steps and contemplated what her plan was…

But should she tell Taylor? That was the one thought she couldn't let go off. Danielle began to have her own suspicions about Taylor. She had thought that she wouldn't actually go out to murder someone. No matter what they had done, even if they had Este's blood on their hands, she never thought that Taylor would actually go through with this. Only at this point grief had consumed her. Danielle scrolled through her phone to look for Taylors number. It wasn't there. She checked once, twice, three times, four. Taylors number didn't exist. And Este's bloody scarf was sitting on the desk across her room. It was clear in view so the sheriff must have seen it.

Danielle got up off the couch and examined the piece of fabric.

"Taylor what have you done."

-Part 9-

Taylor?

Danielle had never done the laundry more frantically than in that moment when she threw the scarf into the washing machine but stopped just as she was about to turn it on, her finger hovering above the button. She pressed it and stood still for a second. Finally everything made sense. It all fell into place. But she couldn't admit it. Taylor hadn't finished her job yet. After all that was the reason Taylor existed, to avenge her *best friend*.

The sheriff was onto it, he knew what was happening and had set up a twenty-four hour, seven days a week watch around Dan's house with almost all his men to watch Dan until they had enough evidence that he killed Este and to keep Danielle away from him. It wasn't easy to pull off but he managed. The watch began the morning he left Danielle's house and Danielle walked past that way to make sure the sheriff wasn't accusing anyone else of Este's murder. Danielle walked on foot, and decided to leave her car at home to get some fresh air after everything that had recently happened. When she reached the diner she walked in and headed straight for the bar.

"Hey Stella, have you seen Taylor recently?" The question was almost innocent, but not quite. The waitress gave the girl a confused look with a half smile.

"Taylor?" She asked, to make sure she heard correctly.

"Yeah, Taylor. You know who Taylor is." Danielle confirmed the name but got nothing more than an awkward chuckle in return, followed by a piece of crucial information.

"I haven't seen Taylor since she closed the shop last year and moved to live with her sister in Tennessee." Stella tried to smile again but looked rather worried and perhaps even a little scared for Danielle.

"No not that Taylor I mean-" She stopped mid sentence when the last piece of the puzzle was finally found.

"There is no Taylor…"

"Danielle are you okay?" Stella walked out from behind the counter to see if everything was okay but Danielle's reaction only freaked her out more than she already was.

"It's me… I'm Taylor." She mumbled under her breath and ran out of the diner back to her house. Stella didn't understand what it was that she muttered to herself but knew that her gut was telling her to call the sheriff. The idea of a "Taylor" subconsciously stemmed from their old friend Taylor who moved away a year ago to live in Tennessee.

Danielle ran into her house, she sprinted and locked the door behind her as soon as she opened it. Taking the scarf from the laundry she put it on. No hesitation was present now that Stella knew. She had to finish what Taylor started.

Although Taylor was just an alter ego Danielle subconsciously created in her mind to get over her grief, it had taken over her. She had created the most elaborate story of them all, all just to get over her sister's passing; Taylor was a coping mechanism and her scarf was what made her Taylor. It was too much for her to handle but she knew what she had to do before the police caught her and sent her into some sort of mental asylum. She would rather sit behind bars knowing she avenged her sister.

First stop was the pawnbrokers. Danielle demanded that Shane give her the axe but he reminded her that the shop no longer has it.

"It was taken in by the police as evidence, remember?" he said. "Are you okay Danielle?"
Danielle ignored his question and further demanded to borrow his shotgun. Of course Shane would never give it to her in such a state. No axe, no gun, that's fine though because Taylor would find her way around difficulties anyway.

Danielle gave into her alter ego and let Taylor consume her completely. She walked to Dan's house with no hesitation whatsoever and hammed her fist at the door. The police car down the block was hidden out of view behind a tree, not that that was anything important however because Officer Dooley was always sleeping on the job - literally. Danielle wanted to knock again but stopped just as her hand was about to touch the surface of the door.

"Get away from me!" She heard Mary shout from inside the house. "It all makes sense now, why you weren't at her funeral, why she wasn't around; why you didn't wear your wedding ring. I'm calling the police." Danielle sneaked a peek through the window where the curtains were open the slightest bit and observed what was happening inside.

"I have a gun and you have a screwdriver. Who do you think will win this fight, Mary? Oh I had such good plans for us Mar… and now I'll have to find someone else to share them with." Dan's tone was almost demonically calm and he sounded just like a maniac. For a moment Danielle thought she was in a horror movie. She paused and thought about what she should do. Mary clearly needed help and obviously she was not involved with Este's murder either. But she wanted to get Dan, not be another one of his victims. She lifted her hand from the door she was only slightly touching and stepped back.

"On three, come on Danielle you went to police academy you can kick down a door." She told herself.

-Part 10-

Dan's Demise

With a bang the door of Dan's house came crashing inwards, Officer Dooley still sleeping atop his steering wheel with a doughnut in his hand at the end of the street. The two heads turned towards Danielle who was now standing in the doorway. Although she looked more like a maniac now, much like Dan. She had a fiery look in her eyes that couldn't mean anything good. The second she laid eyes on Dan fury took over her and she knew she wanted to end it all right then and there. Mary wasn't sure what to do, she stood with her outstretched arm still holding the screwdriver that was pointed at Dan. Her eyes flicked between Dan and Danielle - or Taylor as she was now.

"Two? I guess I could add one more thing to my to-do list today." Dan said as if it was nothing, a casual conversation.

"You're sick." Danielle said after she dropped her raincoat to the floor. "Let her go." The look seeking vengeance was suddenly gone from her eyes.

"Oh but I can't. Well, actually *you* can't. Because after you killed your best friend out of jealousy you had to kill my girlfriend too to make it look like it was me, not you. You're smart, you know that, Taylor." He said with a grin.

"You…" Danielle thought out loud. "You did this to me."

"Of course I did, Taylor-"

"Stop calling me that." She covered her ears through her hair. Poor Mary was still standing, fearing for her life in the living room behind Dan.

"I don't have time for games." Dan said, aiming the gun at Mary while still looking at Danielle. He kept on talking but Danielle half ignored him, instead choosing to help Mary rather than take her revenge just yet. She managed to signal to Mary through subtle hand gestures that Dan hopefully couldn't see to stab him in his right shoulder with which he was holding the gun and then run.

Mary executed the plan well and bolted to the door but unfortunately Dan pulled the trigger just before she got away and shot her in her left leg. Somehow Mary managed to get through the back door and out through the garden. Dan stumbled but managed to maintain his balance but he did let go of his gun which was now sitting on the floor. Much to Danielle's dismay she wasn't quick enough to pick it up before him. Realizing her mistake of not getting a weapon sooner she ran to the kitchen where she took the biggest knife she could find.

"You girls are all so naive. You think you can beat me with a knife?" All I have to do is pull the damn trigger.

"Pull it then!" Danielle yelled, annoyed more than anything else now. "I want to know why you killed her."

"Don't lie to yourself, sweetheart. We both know that's not all you want from me. Otherwise you wouldn't have knocked down that door. You didn't come here to save Mary. You came for me. So go on then, stab me. I dare you."

Danielle threw her knife towards his feet, standing still. "Why did you kill her?"

"Because I wanted to."

"Why?" Danielle pressed, tears welling up in her eyes. No response. A gunshot echoed in the neighbourhood.

Danielle stumbled back clutching her waist, ears ringing as she tried to remain conscious. Dan walked towards her, gun still in his hand, as she laid on the floor, leaning in her left arm. The knife was right there by her hand but she'd rather not make any sudden movements. He towered over her like the leaning tower of Pisa leans over the Doma.

"So pretty... and so naive." He brushed some hair out of her face. That's when she struck. She grabbed the knife and in one swift motion stabbed. Perhaps she had just missed his heart. Perhaps she had punctured his lung. Maybe she got it right in his liver. She wasn't sure, everything began to blend together into a blur from her continuously increasing loss of blood. He fell and she just managed to roll away before he collapsed on top of her. Trying to get to her feet she reached for the white marble worktop in the kitchen, spreading red everywhere she touched it. Blood was dripping from her hands and wound making a breadcrumb trail. Somehow, she pulled herself up and walked the few steps she needed to get to the back door. The door was just within reach. It was open which saved her time and she was ready to step outside when another shot was fired straight into her right leg. She fell through the open door into the grass.

Groaning, she tried to stand but failed miserably. Soon it was Dan's turn to lose his balance and trip through the door. On his hands and knees he coughed up blood into the dirt and grass, the gun never leaving his side. Dan knew he wasn't making it out alive and so did Danielle. He fell to his side and rolled onto his back, lying next to Danielle in his back garden.

"The liver... I knew you wanted more than answers." Danielle's lungs whistled as they began to fail her.

"What did you do to me..?" She coughed, quietly.

"Daily doses of-" he was interrupted by his own coughing, blood dribbling down his mouth. "...Of hallucinogenic drugs. In your food. At Tim's diner... Big enough doses... they'll alter the way you think..."

"You made me a psycho." Danielle pushed herself off the floor and onto her knees.

"Didn't want to be the only one." Dan told her as she leaned over him. He lifted his hand lazily, pressing the tip of the gun against her chest.

"You're more than just a psycho." Her eyes never left his, even though he tried to look away. "You're a maniac." She pulled the knife out of his wound and stabbed him again. A sharp breath rang through the cold air. Danielle fell to her side again and laid there, motionless in the grass. Hope that Mary had alerted the police was vanishing faster than she would have liked.

Bang.

One last shot was fired, from less than twenty centimeters away right into the left side of Danielle's chest.

"I hope... you.... go... to hell."

"I hope… you… you…"

-Part 11-

Flashing Lights

Red and blue illuminated the stillness of the dark street where Este and Dan used to live. Two ambulances, one after the other, raced through the small town of Kohler to the scene while the police had already announced both bodies dead. Dan, with his arm still holding the gun and his head turned to his right, had no more malice in his eyes, but a wicked grin remained plastered on his face. To his right, Danielle's colour had faded from her cheeks, the bright sparkle of her eyes was gone. The town's people swarmed the scene, all with their phones out and bewildered looks on their faces.

Mary sat on the edge of the ambulance wrapped in a blanket. Leg bandaged temporarily and painkillers swimming their way into her system.

"...So he pulled out a knife at me and all I could grab was a screwdriver from his tool box that was on the table. Danielle had knocked the door down, I think... She must have heard us shouting- she must have heard *me* shouting. He wasn't shouting, at all. He was calm, as if nothing was happening as if it was a completely normal situation. It finally all made sense."

"And what happened when Miss Heim came in?" A young officer asked Mary politely.

A couple of meters away, by the sheriff's car, Officer Dooley was getting a lecture from the chief.

"Pathetic. Look what happened on your watch!"

"I-"

"No, No 'I' s no but's no nothing. This is your last chance Dooley!

The two bodies were soon covered for obvious moral reasons. Only the police had made a crucial mistake; they had left the scene unattended for just a moment. One of the white covers started to rustle and something moved beneath it. Dan or Danielle? The latter. Suddenly the cover came off. A very much alive version of Dan sprung up from beneath the white plastic.

He checked the area and made sure he was alone. Then when the time came, he made a run for it and ran into the woods behind the house. When he reached the riverside he stopped for a breath. A bulletproof vest can only stop so much of a stab wound.

"I was wondering how much longer you would take." Este walked out of the Cabin amidst the trees.

"You try running when you've been stabbed three times."

"Oh yeah you can speak, you hit me in the head with an axe, remember."

"Oh right, yes I did, didn't I?" Dan got out of the bullet proof vest and Este took care of the mild wounds.

"Did she not at all question what had happened?" Este asked Dan about Danielle, cleaning the place Mary stabbed him with a screwdriver.

"No," He shook his head. "She was as oblivious as they get."

And it was true. Danielle did not in fact question the convenience of the situation for one second. She acted on thought and plainly wanted revenge, no matter what it took. The poor girl didn't know what was really happening.

When Este and Dan were finished they piled up the last of things in the car and got in, ready to drive away.

"How much did you pack?" Dan asked Este, loading a bag into the trunk.

"Only the bare necessities."

Mary was the one who found Dan and Danielle lying lifeless in the back. She ran back as soon as she managed to get hold of a police officer. It was a sight she will never get out of her head and will haunt her for the rest of her life. But she was glad that she at least got away, and all thanks to Danielle too. For that she blamed herself. She kept telling herself that if she had gotten back sooner Danielle might still be alive and Dan would be in handcuffs being escorted to prison. Her leg wasn't broken or fractured, thankfully the bullet Dan had fired had just missed her calf bone. After the paramedics had temporarily bandaged up her leg, she sat in the back of the ambulance for a while, tightly clutching the blanket she was given, in her hand. A car drove past the scene and she watched it since it appeared at the bottom of the street and disappeared behind her. Police cars and the ambulances mostly blocked the way and the chief had secured the perimeter with that eye irritating "CRIME SCENE DO NOT CROSS" yellow tape, but the car found its way around. The driver was a man. A very familiar man. He looked at her and smirked. From behind him peeked out another head. A woman this time. Mary hadn't seen her. Not in person anyway, only in photos in the house. Mary's chest felt heavy and she felt a cold shiver going down her spine. It took her a moment to realize who it was but when she did she jumped down from the ambulance - a very bad decision which sent a jolt of pain up her leg - and shouted to the chief, running to the back of the house. She ducked under the tape and barged past policemen who wouldn't let her pass.

"He's gone, go after that car!" She shouted. The chief followed her and when he saw the empty space next to Danielle he knew he had to act at once.

"You heard her go after that damn car, move it, move it!" The sheriff shouted.

"How did he get away…" Mary let out a shaky breath, aware that the man who wanted to kill her a couple of hours ago wasn't in fact dead at all. He was very much alive and walking; and as if that wasn't enough, he was on the run too.

"We will get him." The sheriff assured her. "He'll pay for what he has done. To Este and Danielle alike."

"He didn't kill his wife." The sheriff stared at her in disbelief, confused.

"She was next to him in the car. She's with him. She's not dead. The body you buried, it isn't Este. It must be someone else. Or perhaps it isn't a real body at all. But they staged this. All of it. You have to believe me, sheriff. I know you probably want to say I'm just delusional because I just witnessed this but I know who I saw in that car."

"If what you're saying is really true, then we must reopen Este's case and investigate it further. I'll get on the phone to the chief as soon as I can."

"One more thing." Mary turned to him again. "I want to be on the team."

In the car, Dan and Este were checking their list twice.

"You left the security camera footage as it was, right?" Este asked him as he drove onto the highway.

"Yes I did, don't stress me out."

"Well I'm just making sure I didn't die for nothing." Este joked.

"They have the camera footage. But I don't think it will be of any use now that Mary saw us."

"They won't believe her anyway. And if they do then what the cameras captured will just confuse them."

"If they do believe her then what?"

"Then we add one more name to the list."

He did it.

The End.

Original Story by Eliska Belejova, inspired by the original track *"No Body No Crime"* by Taylor Swift.

find me on Instagram & Twitter: @eliskabelejova
support me Redbubble: @boogara
read more on my Wattpad: @LunarSails

Printed in the USA
CPSIA information can be obtained
at www.ICGtesting.com
LVHW051134171223
766705LV00010B/647

9 798849 429373